A TEMPLAR BOOK

First published in the UK
in hardback in 2005
by Templar Publishing.
This softback edition first
published in 2006 by
Templar Publishing,
an imprint of
The Templar Company plc,
Pippbrook Mill, London Road,
Dorking, Surrey, RH4 1JE, UK
www.templarco.co.uk

Copyright © 2005 Cliff Wright

First softback edition

ISBN-13: 978-1-84011-546-8
ISBN-10: 1-84011-546-7

Designed by Cliff Wright
and janie louise hunt

Printed in Hong Kong

Thanks to everyone for
supporting these bears;
to Mandy for not
forgetting them and
to Nadya for not
allowing me to! – C.W.

*THE BEARS
in this book were inspired
by those real creatures
that live in the rainforest of
Western Canada – their homes
are endangered.
If you would like to find
out more, visit;
www.vws.org
or
www.raincoast.org*

Three
BEARS

BY CLIFF WRIGHT

templar publishing

Three Bears
fishing in Black Bear's boat...

hurry for their homes –
Quick! Before the storm breaks.

Rain lashes down. Wind whips wildly, tearing branches from the trees.

Black Bear's boat sinks.

Brown Bear's house blows down –

right on top of Brown Bear.
"Help!" he cries. "My leg hurts."

"Never mind,"
says Black Bear.
"You can come and stay with me."

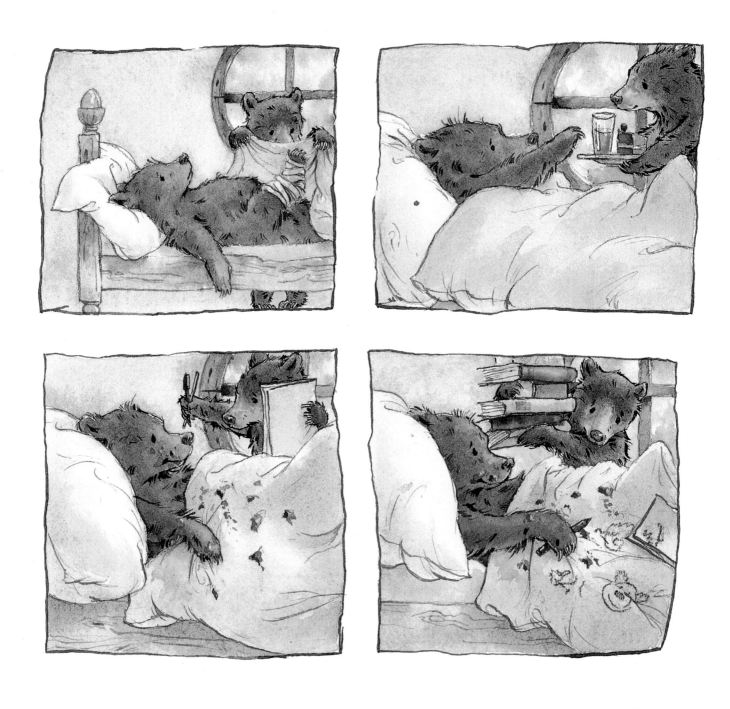

At first, Brown Bear
doesn't mind staying in bed.

Sometimes,
it really is very
nice to be looked after.

But then Black Bear
starts to go out a lot.
Left on his own, Brown Bear
doesn't feel quite so happy.

"What are you doing?" Brown Bear asks.

Black Bear says,
"Oh, um... nothing.
Just going for a
walk with
White Bear."

The more Brown Bear watches,
the more he sees.
And the more he sees,
the less he knows.

What are
the beavers doing with the bears...

and those bits of battered beam?

Why are the
wolves piling up planks and
collecting old chairs?

"I know," says Brown Bear, alone to himself. "They must have a SECRET!"

"They are
building a boat!" he yells.
"A NEW boat,
with a mast and a sail.
A boat with a seat in it for
TWO bears...

...AND NO ROOM
ON IT FOR ME!"

"Oh dear," says Black Bear when they arrive home. "We didn't mean to upset you."

"Would you like to see our secret?" adds White Bear.

After they have
cleared up the mess, his friends take
Brown Bear to show him what
they have really been doing.

And
there is a
new home they
have built him,
in a sheltered
spot out of the wind.

"Ah..." says Brown Bear. Then, "Thank you" he whispers, and he is so pleased that he gives a party that afternoon. When it is finished he stands up and says "I have an idea..."

"Let's build a boat for Black Bear!
A new boat with a mast and a sail.
A boat with a seat in it
for THREE bears!"
And that's just what they do.